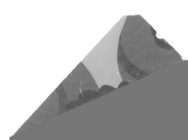

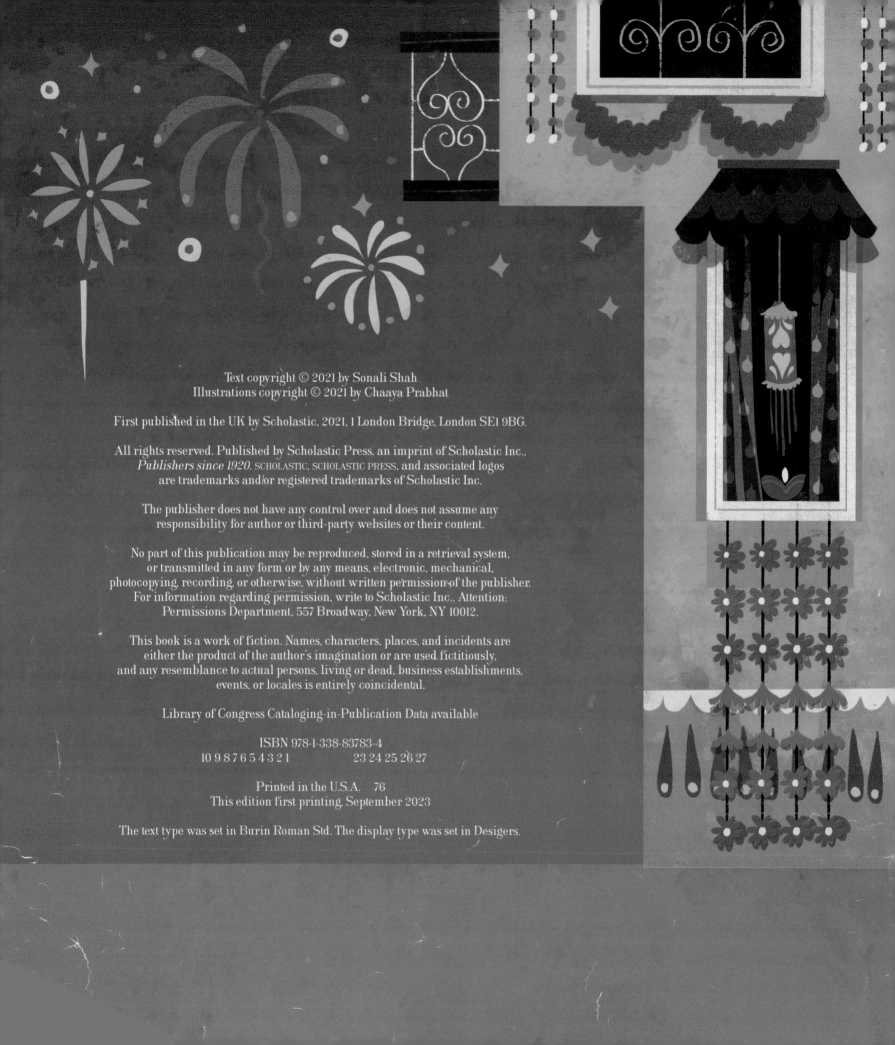

THE BEST
DIWALI EVER

SONALI SHAH

CHAAYA PRABHAT

Scholastic Press • New York

The festival of lights, Diwali, is nearly here. Everyone in my family is getting so excited.

But nowhere near as excited as me.

You see, I have plans to make this year's celebrations **extra** special.

I'll help make yummy sweets,

wear the prettiest clothes ever,

decorate the house with lots of divas,

play with my favorite cousins,

open holiday presents,

stay up late to watch fireworks,

AND . . . this year, I am definitely going to win the rangoli competition.

The only problem is my super-annoying little brother, Rafi.
He's always ruining things — knocking down my building blocks,
losing all my puzzle pieces, and scribbling over my best art.

And no one does anything about it!

"Your brother's only three, Ariana!
That's how you were when you were three."

I don't believe them. There's no way I was that
annoying. But that's what they always say.

On the first day of the festival,
I skip down the stairs to help
my grandmother make the
tasty Indian sweets I love.

The next day, I can't
wait to wear my new
outfit — Mom bought me this
long, rainbow skirt. It's the
prettiest skirt I've ever seen.

But Rafi decides to cover the entire kitchen floor with flour! It takes us so long to clean up.

But then Rafi gives me a big hug — right after he's been doing some finger painting! **Arrrgh!** My brand-new Diwali outfit is **completely ruined**. What a disaster!

We go to the temple to say prayers,
light divas, and watch the dancers.

While everyone is sitting quietly, enjoying the show, Rafi decides to get up and join in the dancing. Right in the middle. With everyone watching. It was so embarrassing . . .

. . . and a little bit funny.

Then we go to my cousins' house — we always have so much fun eating and playing together. Rafi spends most of dinner making funny faces at everyone, and then he throws his food right into my hair!

I'm so mad at him, but I try to forget because . . .

... at last, it's time for the school rangoli competition!
For weeks now I've been practicing creating patterns
with colored powder, rice, and flowers.

This is how my design looks in the end.
I really, **really**, **really** think it's good enough to win the top prize ...

... until my brother falls backward into the powder, rolls over,
and smudges the top of my creation — right before the judges see it!

I huff and puff and all I want to do is cry.
My annoying little brother has ruined everything ...

...again!

But then, the strangest thing happens. Everyone who walks past keeps saying how *beautiful* my rangoli is.

The judges come over and talk about how unusual it looks, especially the top part, before telling me I've won first prize. FIRST PRIZE!

I won because of Rafi's "oops."

As soon as we get home, all our friends and
family start arriving for our big Diwali party.
The house is soon packed full of people talking and laughing.

Thank you, Rafi.

Rafi is playing in the corner.
I go over and give him the **biggest** big sister hug.

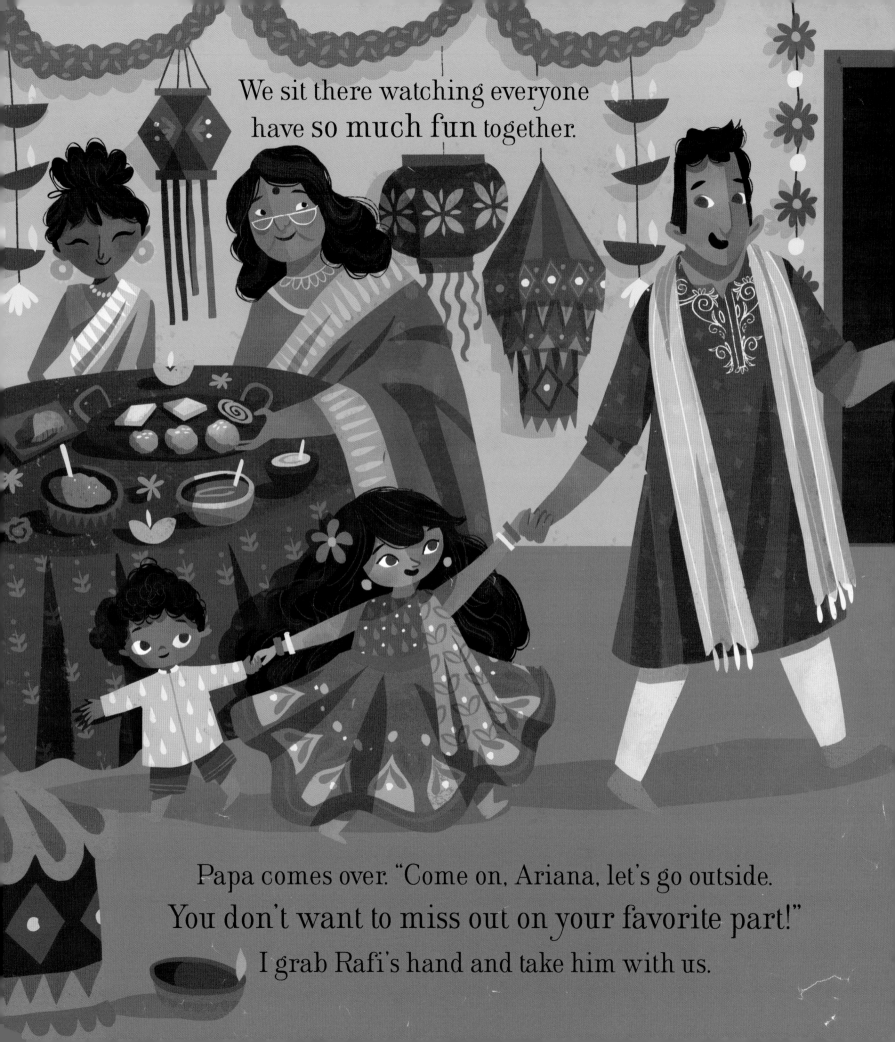

We sit there watching everyone
have so much fun together.

Papa comes over. "Come on, Ariana, let's go outside.
You don't want to miss out on your favorite part!"
I grab Rafi's hand and take him with us.

We look up just as the rockets shoot off and
then burst into round balls of falling stars.

The fireworks bang!

Whiz!

Papa hands me sparklers. "Time to put some gloves on.
I think you're old enough now to hold them." I start making magic
shapes with them, which makes Rafi smile and clap.

"Good job, Ariana!" my brother shouts, making everyone laugh.

That's when I realize: Rafi may be annoying, but
life is actually way more fun with him around …

and he helped make this the best Diwali ever!

Diwali, the festival of lights

Diwali is the biggest religious and cultural festival in India. It is celebrated every October or November by millions of Hindus, Sikhs, and Jains around the world, and thousands of others join in, too. These three religions, which all started in India, have different reasons for celebrating the holiday:

Hindus celebrate the beginning of a new year by honoring their gods and goddesses. They also remember the story of Rama and Sita, who returned home after escaping from an evil king called Ravana.

Sikhs mark the day their sixth Guru, Hargobind Singh, and fifty-two other princes were released from prison.

Jains celebrate the day their founder, Lord Mahavir, reached eternal bliss, or nirvana, and remember his teachings about nonviolence.

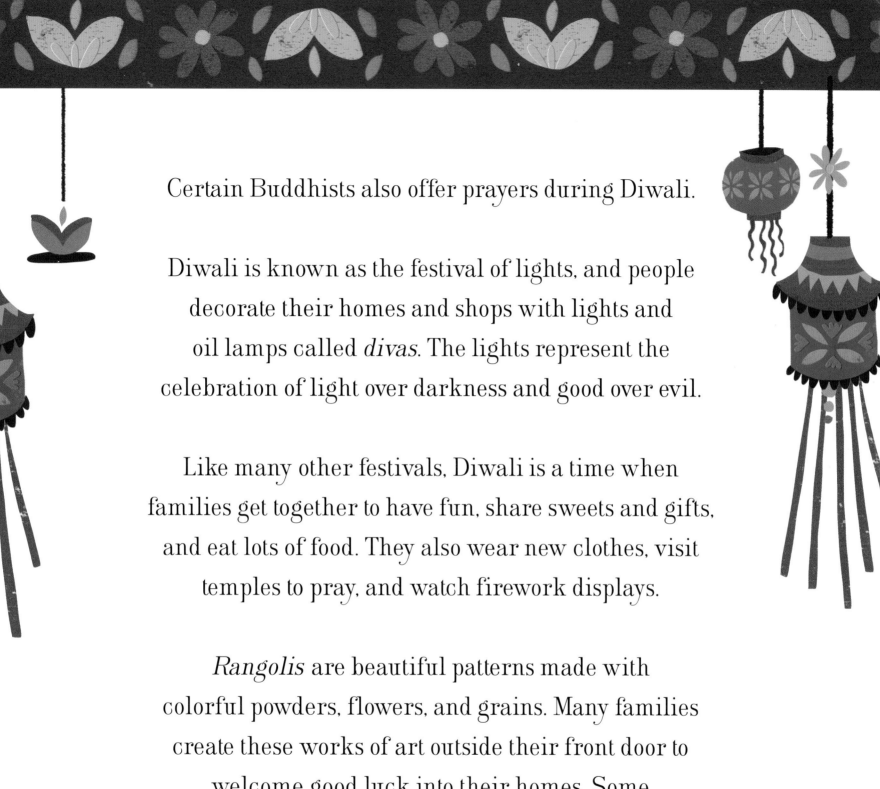

Certain Buddhists also offer prayers during Diwali.

Diwali is known as the festival of lights, and people decorate their homes and shops with lights and oil lamps called *divas*. The lights represent the celebration of light over darkness and good over evil.

Like many other festivals, Diwali is a time when families get together to have fun, share sweets and gifts, and eat lots of food. They also wear new clothes, visit temples to pray, and watch firework displays.

Rangolis are beautiful patterns made with colorful powders, flowers, and grains. Many families create these works of art outside their front door to welcome good luck into their homes. Some communities hold competitions and hand out prizes for the most artistic rangoli designs.